Fitzwarren
Castle

N

W T E

S

Cringleford
Down

The Park

Signpost

Sneaky's
House

Torpedo's
Place

To Wicklewood Forest →

Croaky's
Tree

Tiberius's
House

Winchester
Towers

Witchford

Jumble
Farm

The Woods
(where Sebastian Squirrel lives)

To Puddleduck Green

Gordon's
House

First published by Tiberius Publishing Ltd

Tiberius Publishing Ltd
Common Road
Shelfanger
Diss
Norfolk
IP22 2DR

Written by Keith Harvey
Illustrated by Paula Hickman

A CIP catalogue record for this title is available from the British Library

ISBN 978-1-902604-12-1

Printed in the U.K.

Tiberius
to the
Rescue

Written by **Keith Harvey**

Illustrated by **Paula Hickman**

Tiberius, a little white mouse with big ears and a long pink tail, was going out to the park to meet with his friends Drag, Sneaky Cat and a new friend, Croaky Crow. Tiberius recently met Croaky Crow sitting on top of the signpost looking lost.

Croaky Crow said he was lost because he did not know his left from his right and had been sitting there all day wondering which way to go!

Left   Right

'I had better get a move on or I'll be late,' Tiberius thought,
as he finished putting away the box of cheeseflakes.

The four friends had
arranged to meet at
the signpost and, when
Tiberius got there,
Drag and Croaky Crow
were already waiting.
"Sorry I'm late,"
said Tiberius.

"That's all right,"
said Drag,
"Sneaky Cat hasn't
arrived yet. It is most
unusual for him
to be late."

As they waited, Torpedo the dragonfly hovered past,
Miss Ladybird flew by and Snail crawled slowly down
the path, but there was still no sign of Sneaky Cat.
They waited and waited and waited.

"Do you think he's got lost? I think we had better start a search party," said Drag.

"How do you start a search party?" asked Croaky Crow.
"Simple!" said Tiberius, "Croaky Crow, you fly and see if there is any sign of him around the village. Drag you see if he is still at home. I will go and see if he is down at the park."

So the three friends set off
in different directions in
search of Sneaky Cat.

Croaky Crow flew
around the village but
there was no sign of him.
Drag called at Sneaky Cat's
house but there was no reply.

On his way to the park, Tiberius saw
Georgina, Sir Patrick Fitzwarren's
daughter. She was hopping her way to school.
"Why are you hopping?" called Tiberius.
"I've got a hole in my shoe and I don't want
to get my feet wet, or even worse a wiggly
worm between my toes!" replied Georgina.

Tiberius laughed. "Your feet are too smelly
for a wiggly worm to go between your toes!
By the way, have you seen Sneaky Cat?"
"Sorry, I haven't," said Georgina.
"Fine," said Tiberius "I had better
keep on looking."

Tiberius went off into the park and into the woods,
and looked left and right. Still no sign of Sneaky Cat.
Tiberius was just about to give up to go and meet the others
when he thought he heard someone calling his name.

"Tiberius . . . Tiberius . . . Tiberius!"

Tiberius looked around but couldn't see anybody.
So he called out. "Sneaky Cat, is that you?"
"Oh Tiberius," a voice called out. "I'm stuck at the top
of this enormously high tree and I can't get down.
Please rescue me."

Tiberius looked up and
there, at the top of
the tallest tree in
the wood, was
Sneaky Cat.

"What are you doing up there?" called Tiberius.
"I don't know," said Sneaky Cat,
"but please rescue me as I don't like heights."

"I'll do my best," said Tiberius.
"I'll go and find the others. Don't go away,"
he said with a smile on his face.

Tiberius found Drag and Croaky Crow and they
went back to the woods. They all stood at the
bottom of the tree and looked up at Sneaky Cat.
"How are we going to rescue him?" said Drag.
"I'll fly up and have a word with him," replied Croaky Crow.

Poor Sneaky Cat was shaking as Croaky Crow landed beside him.
"Oh, it's good to see you. How ever am I going to get down from here?"
"Don't worry," said Croaky Crow. "Just try and keep calm
whilst I go down to the others and work out a plan."
"Please don't be long because I don't like it up here
on my own," said Sneaky Cat, sounding a little tearful.

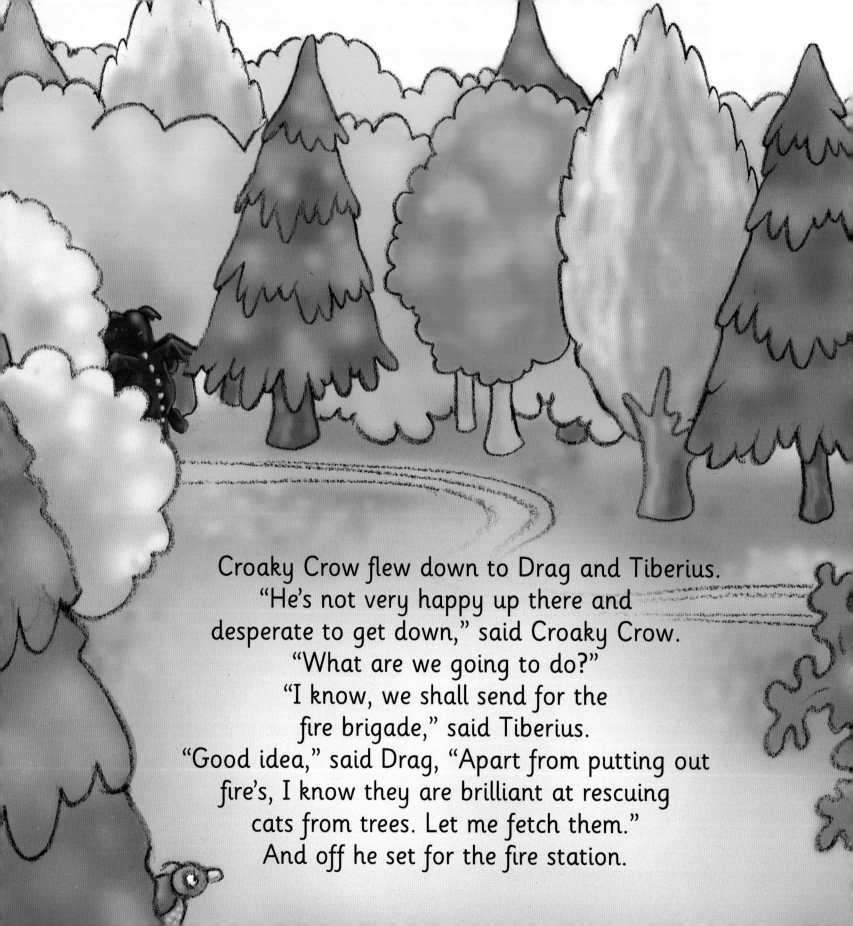

Croaky Crow flew down to Drag and Tiberius.
"He's not very happy up there and
desperate to get down," said Croaky Crow.
"What are we going to do?"
"I know, we shall send for the
fire brigade," said Tiberius.
"Good idea," said Drag, "Apart from putting out
fire's, I know they are brilliant at rescuing
cats from trees. Let me fetch them."
And off he set for the fire station.

Croaky Crow said that he would
fly up and keep Sneaky Cat company.
"Do you think I could fly up there with
you if I sit on your back?" said Tiberius.
"We can try," said Croaky Crow,
"but don't wriggle and hold on very tightly."
Tiberius quite enjoyed the ride on Croaky Crow's back.

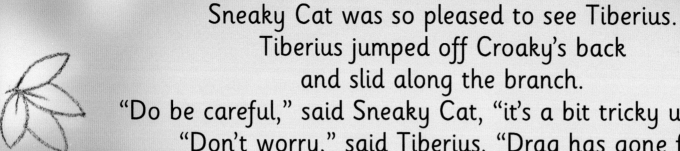

Sneaky Cat was so pleased to see Tiberius.
Tiberius jumped off Croaky's back
and slid along the branch.
"Do be careful," said Sneaky Cat, "it's a bit tricky up here."
"Don't worry," said Tiberius, "Drag has gone for
the fire brigade and you'll soon be safe."

Just at that moment, Croaky Crow saw
his cousin in another tree and promptly flew off
for a little chat. Tiberius saw Croaky Crow fly away
and then he knew exactly how Sneaky Cat felt. It really
was quite scary and very wibbly wobbly as the branches
danced around in the breeze.

Sneaky Cat and Tiberius clung tightly to each other.
"I do wish the fire brigade would hurry up," said Sneaky Cat.
Suddenly they heard a siren. "It's the fire brigade coming!"

Sure enough as they peered through the branches they could see the fire engine zooming along the road.

Drag was sitting in the front with a fireman's hat on and a big smile beaming across his face.
He was obviously enjoying every minute of it.

The fire engine stopped at the bottom of the tree.
The fireman jumped out and looked up.
"We'll have to use our biggest ladder
to reach him, but that's not a problem.
We'll have him down in no time," said the fireman.

The ladder was quickly in place and the fireman slowly and carefully climbed up to the top. Sneaky Cat and Tiberius waited anxiously for him to arrive.

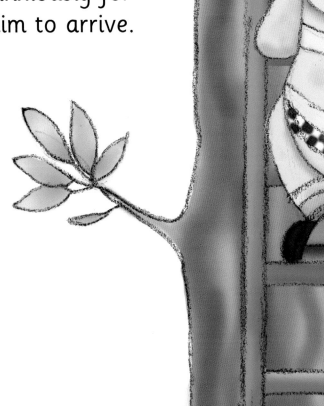

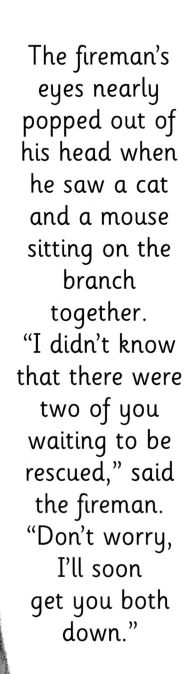

The fireman's eyes nearly popped out of his head when he saw a cat and a mouse sitting on the branch together. "I didn't know that there were two of you waiting to be rescued," said the fireman. "Don't worry, I'll soon get you both down."

The fireman lifted Sneaky Cat onto the top
of the ladder and then reached for Tiberius.
"You won't drop me will you?" squeaked Tiberius. "I know
you are good at rescuing cats, but what about mice?"

The fireman gradually   brought the two of them
down to safety.
Drag, Sneaky Cat and Tiberius thanked the
fireman and went to find Croaky Crow.

When the fireman arrived back at the station he told all his friends how he had rescued a cat **and** a mouse from the top of a tall tree. He said that he knew how the cat could get there, but he couldn't guess how the mouse did.

But we know don't we!